The Church of the Little Saints

Author
Victor Beshir

Illustrations
Sheren Eskander

As an eight-year-old Mark knelt down beside his bed, he said a heartfelt prayer that ended with, "Goodnight, Lord Jesus. I love you."

Afterward, Mark recited the Lord's Prayer
"Our Father who art in heaven . . ."
He closed his eyes and fell asleep.

Not long after, Mark found himself walking through the most beautiful green meadows he had ever seen. He was surrounded by tall trees with many singing birds on the branches, filling the air with pleasant waves of joy. He passed by a creek where he heard pleasent-sounding chirps coming from near and far. Jumping with joy, he was moving from one side of a narrow path to the other. The weather was neither hot nor cold, it was just perfect, making it so inviting to enjoy every moment.

Then, from a distance, he could see a church and could hear songs of worship coming from it. "Wow, I never heard such beautiful melodies," Mark thought aloud. "Let me go and see what is inside this church."

Upon reaching the front door of the church, he found a smiling angel greeting him.

"Do not be afraid! I am an angel, and the angels are friends of children who love our Lord Jesus," the angel stated.

With these words, Mark felt complete calm and ease, and found himself smiling back at the angel.

The angel lovingly explained to Mark, "This is **The Church of the Little Saints.** The children who love our Lord Jesus and who love to be with Him come to this church and spend joyous times with Him."

7

Mark was led by the angel as they walked together into the church. Immediately, Mark noticed a deep silence and reverence in the church. No one was talking to each other, not even whispering. Only the priest's prayers and deacons' chanting could be heard.

He drew his attention to seeing how everyone stood with deep concentration and respect as they looked towards the altar; and even the children were standing too, not sleeping, playing, or talking. "Oh, how amazing! How beautiful this church is! It is full of awe and respect," Mark thought to himself.

Not long after that, Mark caught sight of an angel standing next to each child cheerfully. These were guardian angels.

Mark had never seen angels before. They were so beautiful, tall, and stunning in appearance, dressed in robes, with golden wings attached to their backs, and full of light.

Looking next to him, and to his surprise, he saw an angel standing beside him too. He was so happy to see his guardian angel for the first time. With a big smile on his face, he looked at his angel and smiled, and his angel smiled back at him.

He remembered that his Sunday school teacher told him that each baptized child receives a guardian angel who loves and protects the child and is happy when the child prays earnestly,
and in the church stands respectfully and behaves well.

Mark looked at the angels for a while in amazement and wished that the same tender loving angels could be seen in all churches. But they are only seen here in **The Church of the Little Saints.**

Suddenly, heavenly graceful hymns came to his ears, filling his heart with joy. They had such a touch of beauty.

While Mark was gazing at the young deacons, it amazed him to find how they stood up straight, without moving, or resting on something. No child seemed tired or bored, but to the contrary, they were fully awake, enjoying praising the Lord. They were all singing in harmony as if they all were just one person. While singing, they were listening attentively to each other, which helps them all to be in the same tune together. He noticed that nobody was ahead of the others nor singing louder than others. Surely, no one was screaming to make his voice louder than others.

"Wow, this is fantastic. It is really delightful when every young deacon listens to each other and does the same as the little deacons do here, so all can enjoy such beautiful heavenly hymns," Mark again thought to himself.

He looked towards the wondrous Iconstasis and its fabulous icons. The one icon that attracted him the most was the amazing icon of the Lord Jesus Christ. Mark had never seen a more beautiful icon! While he was gazing at the icon, he remembered how his Sunday school teacher repeatedly recited that the Lord Jesus declares, "**Let the little children come to Me**, and do not forbid them; for of such is the kingdom of heaven." Remembering these words, Mark was exceedingly glad and spent a long time staring at the icon of the Lord.

While he was enjoying gazing at the icon, he heard a deacon singing, "Worship God in fear and trembling." So, Mark closed his eyes and knelt down as all the children did.

17

Then, when all the deacons sang, "Lord have mercy, Lord have mercy, Lord have mercy," all the children stood up cheerfully. Mark's eyes returned to focus on the Lord's icon. His heart was full of joy. For a while, the Lord Jesus overwhelmed him with love.

Mark started to tell the Lord Jesus how he loves Him dearly. He told Him how happy he was to talk to Him. Mark enjoyed talking to the Lord Jesus, telling Him everything about his siblings, his friends, his parents, his school, his troubles with some of his classmates, his pet, and his games. For the first time in Mark's life, he knew how to pray—just to tell the Lord about everything and everyone and talk to Him like you talk to your friend.

19

Although Mark spent a long time talking to the Lord in **The Church of the Little Saints**, it seemed like it lasted only a few minutes, which was not long enough for Mark. He felt that he certainly needed a much longer time to enjoy time with His sweet Lord Jesus.

Mark went to partake of the Holy Communion and every child went too. Mark noticed they walked quietly in a row with their eyes focused on the Holy Body. He approached a child to talk to him. "Oh, hush, please," the child politely whispered, turning his face to look at the Holy Body.

21

So, Mark understood that the time of taking the Holy Communion is not a time for talking with other children. Mark heard the children joyfully singing with the deacons before approaching the priest. He happily did like them.

Mark watched the children, one by one, as they quietly and respectfully approached the priest and took the Holy Communion. Then, each child prayed a small prayer thanking the Lord for having the Holy Communion. Afterward, the children chanted joyfully and praised the Lord from the depth of their hearts. They looked joyful with a big smile on their faces.

When they left to go back to their seats, they did that quietly with great respect. He did not see any child running to his place, since they learned not to run in the church. Mark witnessed this majestic heavenly celebration, which touched his heart. He praised the Lord, saying, "Thank you, dear Lord Jesus. Thank you so much. I love you my Lord Jesus so much."

Suddenly, he felt someone shaking him gently and heard a voice saying, "Get up, Mark; it is time to get ready to go to school."

Mark opened his eyes. To his surprise, he neither found **The Church of the Little Saints**, nor the well-behaved children. He also did not find his beautiful guardian angel. Instead, he found his mother sitting on his bed trying to wake him up.

Before going to school, he looked up to the sky and spoke to the Lord Jesus:

"Thank you, Lord Jesus, for showing me **The Church of the Little Saints**. From the children there, I learned to quietly walk in the church without running, to sing joyfully in harmony with others without screaming, to walk in a row without talking to others, or pushing others, before taking the Holy Communion. I love you, my Lord Jesus."

Mark kissed his mother and said goodbye. He then hurried up to catch the school bus. On that day he had such a fresh feeling. He felt a great joy in his heart that lasted for a long, long, long time.

The Church of the Little Saints is published by

St. Mary & St. Moses Abbey Press

stmabbeypress.com

The Church of the Little Saints is published by

St. Mary & St. Moses Abbey Press

stmabbeypress.com